# Clovis Crawfish
## and Echo Gecko

# Clovis Crawfish
## and Echo Gecko

**Mary Alice Fontenot**

Illustrated by
**Julie Dupré Buckner**

PELICAN PUBLISHING COMPANY
Gretna 2003

*The word "Pelican" and the depiction of a pelican are trademarks of Pelican Publishing Company, Inc., and are registered in the U.S. Patent and Trademark Office.*

**Library of Congress Cataloging-in-Publication Data**

Fontenot, Mary Alice.
    Clovis Crawfish and Echo Gecko / Clovis Crawfish and Echo Gecko ;
illustrated by Julie Dupré Buckner.
        p. cm.
    Summary: Lizette Lizard introduces her bayou friends to her cousin,
Echo Gecko, who repeats everything she hears and who wants to learn
Cajun French.
    ISBN 1-56554-708-X (alk. paper)
    [1. Crayfish—Fiction. 2. Geckos—Fiction. 3. Animals—Fiction. 4.
Bayous—Fiction. 5. Louisiana—Fiction.] I. Buckner, Julie Dupré, ill.
II. Title.

PZ7.F73575 Ckf 2001
[E]—dc21                                                          99-088847

Printed in China
Published by Pelican Publishing Company, Inc.
1000 Burmaster Street, Gretna, Louisiana 70053

*To Johnnie Allen and Judy Buys,*
parrain *and* marraine
*of Echo Gecko*

It was almost summertime in south Louisiana. A warm breeze blew across the bayou where Clovis Crawfish lived. Clovis was sleepy. He crawled down into the round hole in the middle of his mud house and settled himself for a long nap.

High up in the big oak tree, M'sieu Blue Jay squawked, "Chee-*ank!* Chee-*ank!*"

In no time at all, Clovis was back up on the bayou bank. He twirled his whiskers around and clicked and snapped

M'sieu Blue Jay spread his wings and flew away, fast, fast. He knew how hard Clovis could pinch with those sharp claws.

Christophe Cricket was in his house under the root of the big oak tree.

Christophe was still trembling, because he was very scared of M'sieu Blue Jay. He stuck his head out long enough to tell Clovis, *"Merci,"* which means "thank you" in French. Then he rubbed his back feet together, making happy, chirpy sounds.

Denise Dirt Dauber buzzed by and lit on the wet mud on the bayou bank. Denise was collecting mud to build a nest where she could lay her eggs and hatch baby dirt daubers.

Lizette Lizard crawled down and around the trunk of the big oak tree. Right behind Lizette, following her every step, was another lizard, except that it was much smaller than Lizette.

"*Bonjour*, Lizette," said Clovis Crawfish.
"Is this one of your children?"
"This is my *petite cousine*,"
said Lizette. "She is a gecko."

Lizette's little cousin said, "Gecko."
"Hear that, Clovis?" asked Lizette. "She repeats
what she hears. That's why we call her Echo Gecko."
"Echo Gecko!" squeaked Echo Gecko.

"My little cousin wants to learn to *parler français*," said Lizette.

Echo Gecko repeated, *"Parler français!"* which means "speak French."

"Can she talk by herself?" asked Clovis Crawfish.

"Oh yes," said Lizette Lizard. "But she is very shy. She will talk when she gets used to her new friends."

Clovis Crawfish looked at Echo Gecko. "Isn't her tail a little short?" he asked.

"Little short," echoed Echo Gecko.

"Oh yes," said Lizette Lizard. "She broke her tail off, but it's growing back. When geckos and lizards lose their tails, they grow back just like your claw, Clovis, when you lose one."

"Lose one," said Echo Gecko.

Christophe Cricket poked his head out from under the oak-tree root.

"Echo Gecko will have to watch out for M'sieu Blue Jay," said Christophe. "Jaybirds eat lizards."

Echo Gecko screeched, "Eat lizards!" She rolled her eyes and shivered.

Sosthene Snake glided across the water in the bayou. He hissed at Fernand Frog and Théodore Turtle, who were sunning themselves on the old log at the edge of the bayou.

Andrew Armadillo came loping up. He snorted at Sosthene Snake. Water moccasins were no problem for Andrew. He was from Texas, where there were rattlesnakes by the dozen.

Andrew was the only one of Clovis Crawfish's friends who did not have a Cajun-French name.

Bertile Butterfly flew in to look for nectar in the butterweeds blooming on the bayou bank.

Bertile said, *"Bonjour,* Clovis," which means
"hello" in French. "So Lizette's little cousin wants to
learn to speak French?"

"Speak French?" repeated Echo Gecko.

Clovis Crawfish twirled his whiskers. *"Mais oui,"*
he said.

*"Mais oui,"* Echo Gecko said.

Bertile Butterfly fluttered her pretty wings. "She really learns fast," said Bertile.
"Learns fast," said Echo Gecko.
"I know a French song," said Christophe Cricket.

# Je peux parler français

Words by Mary Alice Fontenot

Music by Julie Fontenot Landry

*Translation:*
*I can talk French. I can sing French. I can talk, I can sing,*
*I can talk French.*

"*Chanter français,*" said Echo Gecko.
"*Encore!*" said Clovis. That means "do it again."
Christophe and Echo sang the little song four more times.
René Rainfrog started his rain song: "*J'ai chaud! J'ai chaud!*" which means "I'm hot! I'm hot!"
"*J'ai chaud! J'ai chaud!*" said Echo Gecko.

It began to rain. As soon as the first raindrops splashed in the water, all of Clovis's little friends hurried to find shelter.

When the shower was over, the sun came out again. René Rainfrog, Bertile Butterfly, Lizette Lizard, Christophe Cricket, and Gaston Grasshopper watched as Clovis crawled out of his mud house.

All of Clovis's friends came out except his new friend, Echo Gecko.

"Did M'sieu Blue Jay eat Echo Gecko?" asked Christophe Cricket.

"Echo! Echo!" called Clovis. "Where can she be?"

Clovis and his friends heard a tiny voice repeating, "She be? She be?"

Clovis hurried toward the sound, until he came
to a swamp mallow blooming on the bayou bank.
One of the blooms on the mallow had closed up
tightly. "Echo, are you in there?" Clovis asked.
"In there?" echoed the tiny voice of Echo Gecko

Clovis carefully ripped the bloom open with his
big, sharp claw.

Out tumbled Echo Gecko.

"*Merci,* Clovis! *Bien merci!*" said Echo Gecko. "Thanks a lot!"

"Hear that, Clovis?" asked Lizette Lizard. "She can talk by herself, and she can talk French too!"

# PRONUNCIATION GUIDE

| Cajun French | English | Approximate English Pronunciation |
| --- | --- | --- |
| merci | thanks | mare-SEE |
| bonjour | good day, hello | bonh-JHOOR |
| petite cousine | little cousin | puh-TEET coo-ZEEN |
| parler français | speak French | par-LAY frohn-SAY |
| mais oui | but yes | may wee |
| je peux | I can | juh puh |
| chanter | sing | shonh-TAY |
| encore | again | awnh-KOR |
| j'ai chaud | I'm hot | jhay sho |
| bien merci | many thanks | bee-YENH mare-SEE |